Monso

Written by Pam Rushby

Illustrated by Christina Forshay

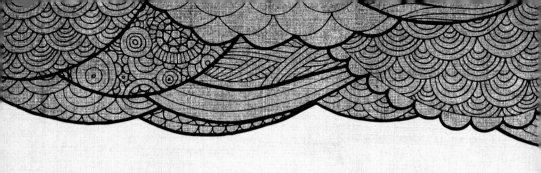

It is getting hotter.
The rainy season is about
to start.
The monsoon is coming.

The rains will be good.
They will help cool the air.
The boy and girl wait
for the rains.

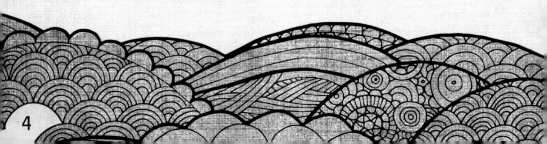

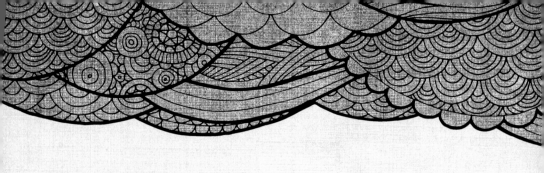

The boy and girl
feel a breeze.
It feels so good!
It helps cool the air.

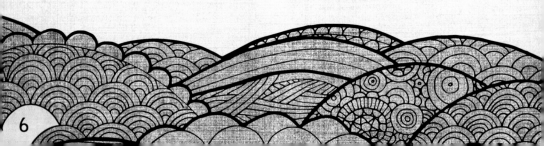

Then, the breeze turns
into wind,
and the monsoon starts!
The rain helps cool the air.
It feels good
to the boy and girl!

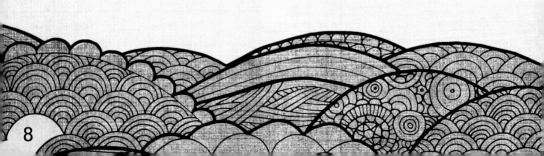

Then, the drain blocks up.
A big puddle forms.
That is not good.

"Help clear the drain,"
the girl calls to the boy.

The boy helps,
but the puddle gets bigger.

"Could it flood our homes?"
the boy asks the girl.

That is not good.

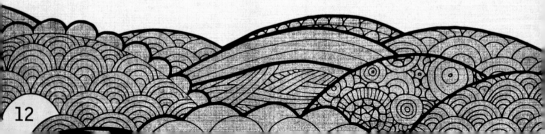

The boy and girl
ask for help.
Good neighbours
help the boy and girl
clear the drain.

The puddle is gone!
That is good!
They all helped stop a flood.